Young & Eager

Barely legal but hardly innocent

"Two Brothers" -- *A divorcée in a flashy sports car attracts the attention of two young virgin brothers visiting the "big" city of Boise.*

"Teachers Pet" -- *Trapped at an all-girls' school in the middle of nowhere, Sabrina tries to get her hunky teacher to bust her cherry.*

"Arresting Development" -- *Bethany went out with Officer Rick to avoid a speeding ticket, but discovered she enjoyed getting "arrested."*

"Jail Bait" -- *Serena wants Joshua to pop her cherry, but he won't touch her because of her age. When her birthday finally makes it legal, he arranges for a very special celebration.*

I.G. Frederick trades words for cash, specializing in erotic fiction and poetry since 2001. Her erotic short stories appear in Hustler Fantasies, Forum, Foreplay, and Desire Presents, as well as electronic, audio, and print anthologies. Her novels receive high praise from readers, critics, and other authors.

A FemDom, Ms. Frederick, owns the man she adores. Although dominant in the rest of his life, he demonstrates his love by serving as her submissive. Ms. Frederick often writes about finding love in BDSM relationships from the authority of one enjoying that for almost a decade.

http://eroticawriter.net/

Young & Eager

Barely legal but
hardly innocent

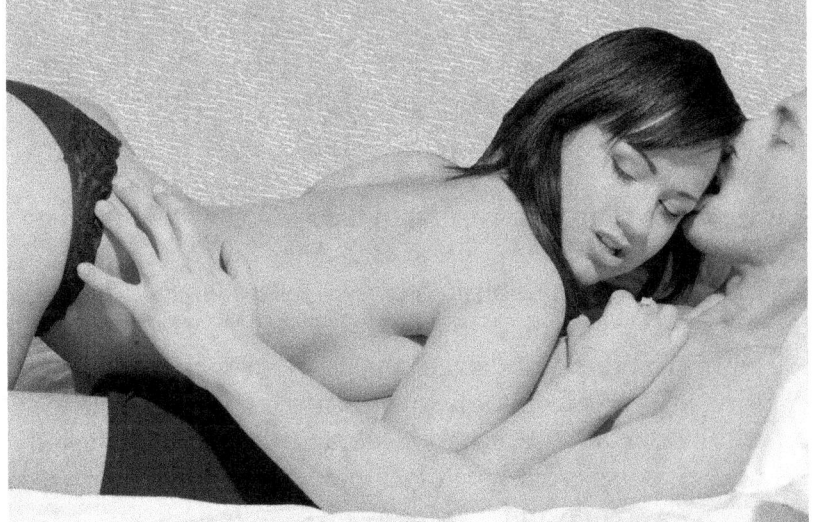

Four Sexy Stories

I.G. Frederick
Author When Two's Not Enough

Young & Eager
© **2014 by I.G. Frederick**

ISBN: 978-1937471-25-5

Pussy Cat Press
http://pussycatpress.com/publisher.html/
P.O. Box 19764
Portland OR 97280

First published electronically in 2011

"Two Brothers" first published in Blue Moon's *MILF Anthology: Twenty-One Steamy Stories,* June 2006
"Teacher's Pet" first published by *Hustler Fantasies,* Aug., 2005

Table of Contents

Two Brothers

By I.G. Frederick

After dropping the kids off at their father's house for one of his weekend visitations, I stopped for paint and wallpaper. I planned to redecorate my children's rooms while they were gone, rather than repeat last month's fiasco. That weekend, instead of taking advantage of my freedom from soccer games and birthday parties to do needed repairs, I spent the entire time surfing the Internet. A visit to an erotica short story website proved barely titillating so I spent hours taking those free tours of porn sites (I couldn't bring myself to give up the personal information required to join). The weekend ended in a frenzied search for cookies and browser history files to erase, so my computer genius son wouldn't find out what his mother had been doing in his absence.

As usual, I parked my cherry-red convertible at the far end of the lot, hugging a landscape island, to avoid getting her dinged. Rita still looked as sharp as when I drove her off the lot the day after my divorce was final, four years ago. Holding the button that raised the ragtop and clicking the fastenings in place, I noticed two young men hanging out next to a battered pickup truck with the hood up. They gave us the once over as I climbed out. I knew they looked mostly at the car. I'm almost forty-five and, although I try to keep in shape, childbearing did take its toll and my hair already shows streaks of grey. Still, I could feel the young men's eyes turn from Rita and follow me through the parking lot. They probably wondered how an old mom got such a sharp ride. I swayed my hips provocatively to let them know that while not young, I'm not dead either. I wore tattered cut offs and an old t-shirt -- great for painting, but hardly sexy. But, they were tight and showed off what I like to call a voluptuous figure.

I forgot about the boys while I shopped, and was surprised to see them when I pushed my cart -- filled with paint, wallpaper, detergent, and other household necessities -- back out to my car. The truck's hood had been lowered and they each rested a foot on the rear bumper. I gave Rita a quick once-over to make sure they hadn't taken their frustration out on my baby. When your husband of fifteen years leaves you for his twenty-two-year-old, size-two secretary, you take whatever consolation you can get -- in my case a sporty, red, five-speed that guys drooled over. I opened the trunk and puzzled about how to squeeze in the cart's contents. Out of the corner of my eye, I saw the shorter of the two men nudge the taller until he ambled over and helped me stow my purchases. Better than six feet tall and all muscle, he wore tight, worn blue jeans, scuffed cowboy boots, and a red, checked cotton shirt that clung to his skin. He smelled of engine oil, sweat, and hay.

I slammed the trunk and turned to thank him. He looked down at me with his wide-brimmed cowboy hat in his hands, his face rugged and tanned as if he spent most of his working days outside.

"Excuse me, ma'am, can I ask you a very personal question?" He shifted his weight from one foot to the other. Maybe he'd never seen a cherry-red convertible driven by a 45-year-old divorcée.

I nodded, curious.

"You see, ma'am, my brother and me are from Lima, Montana, and we've never been to the big city before." Somehow I'd never thought of Boise, Idaho, as the big city. "Before he died, my pappy told us that the first time we got laid we should find a woman with some experience 'cause she would show us how to do it right. We're both still virgins, and we were wondering if you might be interested in teaching us."

My mouth dropped open. I fell against the trunk, but jumped back up when the sun-heated metal burned bare legs below my cutoffs. Well, I had to give him points for originality -- I had never heard a pickup line like that.

His eyes stayed glued to the toes of his boots. "I know this is a little abrupt and I beg pardon, but we noticed you weren't wearing a wedding ring, and we thought maybe a woman who drove a car like that," he pointed his hat at Rita, "and walked the way you do might be," he cleared his throat, "might be more willing than most to consider breaking us in."

I just stared at him, working my eyes down his muscular chest to the crotch of his jeans. A decent size bulge, but he could have stuck socks in there. I don't know if pheromones, the fact that I hadn't had sex with a man in four years, or the heat, made me decide to play along, for the moment.

"Well, now, that would depend on what you had to offer." I kept my voice low and husky and ran one finger along his zipper. The bulge grew and his face turned bright red.

He cleared his throat again. "I believe, ma'am, that I may be a little bigger than normal, but I really have no way of knowing."

"What about your brother?"

"He's not as big as I am, ma'am."

I looked at the other young man, shorter and more wiry than his brother, watching us from under his hat. I thought about dated wallpaper and peeling paint as well as long lonely nights alone with a rubber dong -- afraid to use a vibrator because the kids might hear it.

"I'd have to really see what you had to offer before I agreed to anything." I couldn't believe I said that.

He shifted his weight again and scanned the area. Cars were filling the lot. "If you came over to the truck, I could stand behind the door. You and Pete could block the view and I could ... give you a peek."

I envisioned the two of them throwing me in the pickup and taking me somewhere to rape me.

But then why ask? Intrigued, I walked with him over to the truck. Pete and I stood side by side next to the open driver's side door. The young man, he couldn't have been much more than 19, stood with his back to the truck's interior, pulled down his zipper and extracted the longest, thickest cock -- even only half-erect -- I have ever seen in real life. I reached out and ran my finger along the bottom. It stood at full attention -- eight inches long and almost two inches thick. I decided I wanted to be the first woman to sit on it.

I looked up in the man's face and saw his eyes for the first time. A piercing blue, they stared right through me, as if he could see how much I needed a man's touch again.

"Where you boys staying?" I asked.

"We just got into town this morning, and haven't found a place yet." He stood there with his cock hanging out of his jeans. "We stopped here to get some oil for the truck."

I could see remnants of hay bales strewn about the pickup's bed; they'd probably slept in there for a couple of nights. I turned around toward the highway and heard the sound of a zipper closing behind me. "There's a halfway decent motel over by the interstate exit." I pointed in the general direction. You could see the sign from where we stood. "You boys go over there and get a room. I'll follow." I wasn't about to take these fellows home -- I figured I risked enough going to a motel with them. Pete walked around and climbed into the passenger side. I looked up at his brother. "Do you have condoms?"

He shook his head.

"Well, go in the store and get some. I'll wait in my car."

"Uh, ma'am, how many should we get?"

I smiled. I should give these boys a lesson to remember. "At least a dozen, maybe two -- 12 for each of you. And while you're there, get some lube."

His big grin revealed even teeth, white against his sun-darkened face. "Yes, ma'am!"

"My name is Audrey. Please don't call me ma'am any more."

"Yes, m... Audrey. I'm Paul." He extended his hand. "Pleased to make your acquaintance, Audrey."

I put my hand in his big, calloused palm, but instead of shaking, he lifted it to his lips and kissed my fingertips. I guess they watch old movies in Lima.

He and his brother loped into the store. They returned to the truck -- with a very full plastic bag -- less than ten minutes later. I started Rita's engine, lowered her top, put her in gear, and killed the motor with too much clutch. My sensible self screamed at me to scurry home, but as much as I feared trouble, I also couldn't remove the image of Paul's huge cock from my mind.

The boys waved to me, jumped into their truck, and headed back toward the interstate. I waited in the parking lot across from the motel while Paul went into the office. I'd completely lost my mind. Couple of barely legal kids, they probably would get off the minute I let them touch me. Despite my doubts, I followed the pickup to the back of the motel, found a safe parking spot in a corner, and raised Rita's top. I took a deep breath -- last chance to back out -- but climbed out of the car and walked toward the room.

The minute we stepped inside the room, Pete grabbed me, pawed my breasts, and planted sloppy kisses on my mouth. He reeked as if he hadn't bathed in several days. For a moment I panicked, then I pushed him away. He didn't resist and I relaxed a little.

"First lesson -- never grab a woman. Lovemaking should be slow and gentle. Now, I want to know the truth. Are you boys really virgins?" They both blushed. I was charmed.

"Yes, m... Audrey," Paul stuttered. "Neither of us has ever been with a woman before."

I am going to enjoy this so much, I thought.

"Okay, I want you boys to each take a shower. And I want you to jack off while you're in there." They looked at me, eyes wide, mouths opened. I softened my voice. "If you've never been with a woman you're likely to come the minute you get inside me. Not much fun for me." They still stood there staring and shaking their heads. I slapped Paul on the rump. He jumped, but headed for the bathroom, closing the door behind him.

"Leave it open. I want to watch." He stared at me again, then pulled off his clothes.

I couldn't see an ounce of fat anywhere on his body, every muscle was defined under his sun-darkened skin. The tan stopped at his waist, but his legs looked as powerful as his chest and arms. His prick stuck straight out. I stepped into the bathroom and pulled the opaque shower curtain back a little.

When he was all soapy, Paul stroked his lovely cock while staring straight at my tits. I pulled the t-shirt over my head, dropping it on the floor, and unfastened my bra. He shot his load as soon as my double-D cups (hey, I've nursed two kids) fell out of the lace. Paul spurted across the shower and hit the opposite wall. He blushed again and turned his back so he could rinse off.

The minute Paul got out of the shower to towel dry, Pete stripped and stepped in. Not as well endowed as his brother, his dick was nothing to be ashamed of. Although wiry where his brother was thick, Pete looked just as strong. It didn't take him as long to jack off. His load didn't reach the wall either.

With both of them now clean and naked in the room, I hesitated. I was so wet, I could have taken either of them right then and there. But they wanted a teacher, and I wanted to make sure they didn't get by on their physical endowments -- that they learned how to treat women right. I took Paul's hand and led him to one of the double beds. Pulling back the covers, I pushed him gently until he sat down on the sheets. I took his face in my hands, and leaned down to kiss him. I smiled inwardly; he tasted of breath mints.

I teased his tongue with mine, luring it into my mouth. Reaching down, I put his hands on my bottom. He massaged my ass for a few minutes then, slid his big hands up along my back and down across my shoulders to my breasts. While he fondled them, I moved my head so his mouth found its way down my neck. He had learned the first lesson well -- his lips traveled very slowly along the sensitive skin, across my collarbone to my breasts. He moaned when he got my nipple in his mouth and I could see his cock rising again. I ran my fingers through his hair.

"Here, you need to pay attention to the woman you're with and adjust to her preference." I was panting, but they expected me to teach. "Some women like you to be rough with their tits, biting their nipples and sucking hard. Me, I prefer soft nibbles and licking." Paul wrapped his tongue around my nipple, making me groan. I unbuttoned my shorts and pushed them and my wet underpants to my hips.

Moving his mouth to my rounded belly, Paul pulled my clothing down around my ankles. I stepped out of them and lay on the bed, my legs dangling over the side. I pulled Paul's head down and pushed him toward my soaked pussy.

"You can never go wrong eating a woman's pussy boys. If she isn't ready, that will get her wet. If she's having second thoughts, they'll disappear. And, she's liable to return the favor."

I couldn't see Paul's face, but Pete, stood in the bathroom doorway, staring at us, eyes wide, mouth open, cock hard.

Paul buried his face in my pussy, licking on my clit until I bucked up against his face, an orgasm washing over my entire body. I wrapped my legs around his head, pressing my cunt against his mouth.

When the spasms stopped, I lay limp. My legs slid down Paul's shoulders. He lifted his head, his face dripping with my pussy juices, and looked quite pleased with himself. I tugged on his hair and he kissed his way back up my body, stopping for a while at my breasts but finally finding his way back to my mouth. I sucked my juices off his lips. His cock pressed against my thigh.

"Hand me one of those condoms, sweetie." Without releasing my lips, Paul grabbed the plastic bag, and although he spilled most of the contents on the floor, he eventually presented me with one foil packet. I pushed him back, ripped open the wrapping, and rolled the sheath down his magnificent shaft.

"When you first enter a woman, you want to take it slow -- especially someone as big as you. You can use your hand to guide it inside her."

I put my feet on his shoulders, opening my thighs wide so Paul could see. He took his cock in his right hand and, with an adorably serious look, eased it into my wet cunt. He groaned and his expression changed to one of ecstasy. His eyes closed and he slid deep inside. I felt as if he was splitting me in two. I slid my legs down his chest, wrapped them around his back, and tightened my grip to keep him from moving. When I felt comfortable with all that meat, I dropped my feet to the bed and pushed against him. He took the hint and moved in and out. I almost wept from the intensity of the sensations bombarding me.

"Now, here again you should follow the woman's lead," I had a hard time keeping my voice steady. "Some women like it slow and easy like this. Others want you to slam it into them, hard. I'm one of those."

Paul didn't need any more explanation. He pulled his

hips back and rammed me with a force that shook the bed. He found a hard, steady rhythm. My tits bounced around, and his balls smacked against my rear. I cried out as the second orgasm took over, my entire body shaking. I opened my eyes just in time to watch the delight cross his face when my pussy clenched around his shaft. He thrust harder and my orgasm didn't stop until he spasmed.

When he started to pull away, I wrapped my legs around his back. "Never pull it out, hon, unless you come before she does. Then you need to get down there with hands or mouth right away and bring her off. But if you've done it right, you want to stay inside as long as you can."

Paul kissed me. His eyes widened again when he realized my pussy continued to spasm. "Are you still coming?"

"No, it's kind of like the aftershock of an earthquake. If the orgasm is intense enough, the pussy will keep twitching for quite a bit. One reason not to pull out too soon." I smiled up into intense blue eyes and deepened my voice. "That way you can enjoy it, too."

Paul grinned.

"What about me?" Pete's voice trembled. *Poor baby, watching big brother have all the fun.* As soon as Paul softened and slipped out, I pushed at his chest and he rose to his feet. I sat up and patted the bed and Pete didn't waste time accepting my invitation. He started to grab me again, but then hesitated, gently wrapped his arms around me, and kissed me. I wondered if Paul had as little experience as he claimed. Pete's kisses, unlike Paul's, were sloppy and clumsy. I pulled back. "More lip, less tongue, sweetie," I whispered, "and try to keep your saliva to yourself." I suspected everything had been staged to get little brother's cherry popped. Then I remembered the look on Paul's face when he felt my pussy wrapped around his cock -- definitely his first time.

I put one of Pete's hands on my breast. He squeezed it gently -- at least he paid attention -- and leaned down to take the nipple in his mouth. He was breathing heavily and I wondered if the boy would last until he got inside me. I pushed him back on the bed, and sat on his face. Unlike his brother, Pete apparently, knew nothing about female anatomy.

I lifted myself off and looked down at his wet face. "Do you know what a clitoris is, honey?" He looked chagrined and shook his head. "It's the most sensitive part of a woman's body. Very few women can orgasm if you don't stimulate their clitoris in some way." I pulled my nether lips apart and showed him. Pete needed no more instruction. He dove right in, licking and sucking my nob until I shuddered and came all over his face.

I grabbed a condom off the night stand and slid down Pete's chest -- leaving a trail of my juices in the thick mat of hair -- until I felt his erect cock against my butt. Straddling his thighs while I sheathed him, I watched his face. He bit his lip, probably trying to avoid coming too soon. I figured I'd get a head start and grabbed his cock, rubbing it against my clit. His eyes rolled back in his head and he groaned. Without releasing him, I raised myself up and positioned the head of his dick between my cunt lips. I lowered myself, staring at his face. Pete's eyes opened wide and his lips parted, revealing perfect white teeth. I moved up and down his shaft, and he reached up to cup my breasts in his hands, teasing my nipples between his thumbs and forefingers. Bucking his hips he adjusted his rhythm until it matched my own. I rubbed my clit against him with the down stroke and lost control when the throbbing between my legs traveled the length of my body. Pete's hands slid down and grabbed my ass, moving me up and down as he thrust into me. He lasted longer than I expected and when he did come, he screamed so loudly I worried someone would complain to the management.

I collapsed on his chest and we lay there, panting, until he popped out. I rolled onto my back, and before I could think about what to show them next, Paul lay beside me, kissing me and playing with my tits. His hard cock pressed against my hip. Doing them one at a time created a problem, I decided. The other one got aroused again watching me with his brother. At this rate, exhaustion would kill me before lunch. Time to try out one of my all-time favorite fantasies.

"How'd you boys like to both fuck me at the same time?"

Two pairs of wide-open blue eyes stared at me. I pushed off the bed, threw a condom at each of them, and rummaged through the bag to find a large tube. While they tried to get the rubbers on, I slathered my fingers and lubed up my ass. I had Paul lay in the middle of the bed and smeared lube all over Pete's only semi-hard cock. How the hell he had managed to get the condom on, I didn't know. When he was hard and well-lubricated. I eased myself down onto Paul's gorgeous shaft and leaned forward on my hands, putting my ass in the air.

"Okay, Pete, put it in SLOWLY."

I sensed no movement behind me and finally Paul shouted. "In her ass dickhead, she wants you to fuck her in the ass." He lowered his voice. "You should have let me have the back end."

"Sorry sweetie, you're way too big for me to take that way."

Pete pulled my butt cheeks apart with his hand and pressed the head of his penis against my asshole. I relaxed and he slid it partially in, then hesitated. "You're doing fine, hon. Just ease it in nice and slow." I closed my eyes enjoying the sensation of being completely filled from both ends. Paul waited until Pete had sunk in all the way to his balls and then he moved up and down inside me. Pete eased himself almost all the way out and then pushed back in. I just held still, eyes closed, getting thoroughly fucked. Pete reached around and played with my tits. Paul massaged my clit with his thumb. I had to concentrate to keep my arms straight as wave after wave of orgasm pulsed through me. Just a mass of over stimulated nerves, I could no longer see -- no longer hear myself screaming. I'm didn't even notice the boys getting off, but suddenly they both lay still and I could feel them softening inside me.

"This end you need to pull out of, Pete, just do it slowly, please." When he inched himself free from my now very sore asshole. I dropped, managing to land next to Paul's legs instead of on top of them. I pressed myself along Paul's side with my head on his shoulder and my arm across his chest. Pete plastered himself along my backside and let his hand rest on my waist. We panted and I drifted in a post orgasmic stupor, my pussy muscles throbbing incessantly.

By the time our breathing returned to normal, I could have fallen asleep, but I wanted an answer to the question that had been nagging at me all morning.

"Paul, how is it you seem so much more knowledgeable than Pete?"

"I had a buddy in high school whose dad worked for some high-tech firm in San Francisco. They had satellite Internet and when his dad travelled we would check out some," he cleared his throat and I could see a tinge of red creeping up from his neck, "very educational, adult sites."

I laughed. Paul's stomach rumbled, followed immediately by grumbling from Pete's belly. I looked at the clock -- almost noon. I had Pete find the phone book and we called up the first Chinese restaurant listed that delivered. I wanted to make sure my boys kept up their strength. They still had lots more condoms and I had oh so many more positions to show them. And I couldn't wait to watch their faces when I gave them their first blow jobs.

Teacher's Pet

By I.G. Frederick

I'd finally gotten freakin' fed up. My folks had kept me imprisoned in this horrid all-girls' boarding school, a million miles from anywhere interesting, for almost four years. Now, two months past my eighteenth birthday, I was still a virgin and bored out of my skull. Worse, I had twelve more weeks before school ended and I could finally get out of here.

I totally couldn't take it anymore and I had do *something*. Most of the teachers and staff -- middle-aged old maids -- had nothing better to do in life than preach to a bunch of rich bitches about noblesse oblige, chastity, and honor. Dull stuff like that. The only men at the entire school, except for the repulsive maintenance guy, were two male teachers: Mr. Meyers, probably old enough to be my great grandfather, and Mr. Lawrence. One of the youngest teachers, even though almost forty, Mr. Lawrence was six feet tall and very muscular, with straight, thick black hair. His piercing blue eyes could stare right through you -- especially if you didn't have the answer to one of his questions about American History. All the girls

13

had wet dreams about Mr. Lawrence. I had no idea why such a hunky guy would bury himself up here in the woods with a bunch of wrinkled spinsters and a herd of ripe females he couldn't touch. I decided for my Spring project to get Mr. Lawrence to bust my cherry.

I had History last, right after gym. I started not putting on any underwear after I showered. Not that you could tell -- what with the stupid uniforms we had to wear that all but hid the fact that we were female. Then, I pretended to fall asleep in his class. Actually, half the time I didn't have to pretend -- History was probably the most boring subject I'd ever had to take, except maybe for English. But I'd tried pretty hard all year, as did most of the girls -- we all wanted Mr. Lawrence to like us.

Well, after about a week of falling asleep, or pretending to, halfway through his class, Mr. Lawrence finally asked me to stay after. Just the opportunity I needed. He had me sit in the chair beside his desk and he folded his hands in front of him on top of his desk calendar. I thought about those long fingers caressing my jugs and I could feel myself getting wet. If this didn't work, I knew I'd spend a lot of time playing with myself tonight.

"Sabrina, is something wrong?" He had serious creases between his dark, bushy brows and his full sensuous lips turned down.

"No, why?"

"Because until recently you've been a fairly good student." His deep sexy voice sent chills down my spine. "You've fallen asleep in class every day this week. That's just not like you." Little did he know.

"Maybe, I just stopped caring." I tried to sound flip. I wanted to get him pissed at me.

"But, why, Sabrina? What's changed?"

Well, I had no intention of telling him that, so I just shrugged my shoulders.

He sighed, heavily, like he really worried about me. *He should worry about himself.*

"I'm afraid if you don't have a reason for your behavior, I have no choice but to punish you. What do you think would be appropriate punishment for someone who falls asleep in class, Sabrina?" They really do talk like that at this school. Repulsive, but it gave me my opening.

"I think I should have to give you a blow job."

Mr. Lawrence gasped. "Sabrina!" He pushed back in his chair.

I just grinned and propped my feet up on his desk. My plaid, below-the-knee-length skirt fell back and he got a good look at my blonde bush.

"Sabrina, put your feet down immediately! And, why aren't you wearing any underwear?"

"'Cause it just gets all wet when I'm in your class, Mr. Lawrence." I pulled my feet down from the desk and stood up. Before he could stop me, I'd straddled his legs with my thighs and sat in his lap. He tried to protest, but I put one hand on each of his cheeks and pressed my lips to his. With his hands around my waist, he tried to lift me off his lap. But my tongue found its way past his teeth and instead of pushing me away, his arms slid around me. I mean, I'm not too bad to look at: long blond hair, sparkling green eyes, pert tits, and a nicely shaped ass. And, unlike most of my classmates, I'm no longer jail bait. Oh, he probably could still get in plenty of trouble for messing with a student, but at least he couldn't get arrested.

Mr. Lawrence's tongue followed mine back into my mouth and I sucked on it greedily. I wondered what it would be like to suck on his dick instead. I didn't enjoy being a cock teaser, but my folks kept such tight tabs on me when I went home for the summer that frenching was about as far as I'd gone. I didn't worry, though. I'd done plenty of reading. We all had computers with Internet connections in our rooms. They had filters on them, to keep us from getting to any "adult" web pages. I had absolutely no trouble figuring out how to disable them. I also knew how to find all the best free sites with erotic stories and even porno pictures.

With a big hand on either side of my face, Mr. Lawrence pulled my mouth away from his. "Sabrina, I'm very flattered, really I am." He was breathing heavily and I could feel his boner through his slacks against my crotch. "But this isn't right, you know it isn't." His blue eyes stared through me, although they looked a little glassy. His hands slid down to my shoulders and he pushed me off his lap. He seemed to breathe a little easier when we no longer touched. "I'm sure there's someplace you're supposed to be now?" He'd forgotten all about my punishment.

I shook my head and walked toward the door. I swayed my hips from side to side, knowing he would watch. Instead of leaving the classroom, I turned the bolt, pulled down the rolled shade that covered the window in the door, and flicked off the fluorescent overheads. The late afternoon sun, coming in through the windows along the wall, gave me enough light for what I planned. Since the classroom was on the third floor, I didn't think I needed to worry about anyone getting an eyeful.

When I got back to his desk, Mr. Lawrence stood and his jaw had a determined set to it. "Sabrina, I don't know what you think you're doing, but nothing can happen here."

I didn't say a word. I just took his hand and slid it under my green wool sweater and plain white blouse up to my naked breast. He gasped for the second time and sat down rather abruptly in his chair. He looked somewhat defeated and didn't speak when I knelt down, undid his belt, unzipped his trousers, and pulled out his prick. I'd never seen one for real before. It looked just like the pictures, but I was fascinated with how soft the skin felt, especially around the head. At first, I just ran my fingers around the shaft, tickling the head with my nails. I began to have second thoughts -- it was SO big. When I played with myself, two fingers seemed tight. He was way bigger than two fingers. I could barely wrap my hands around him and even with both hands I couldn't cover the length of his shaft.

Mr. Lawrence was panting and I didn't want him to get discouraged while I debated if I was going through with my plan, so I kissed the head of his cock. It kind of jumped at me and he moaned so softly I almost didn't hear him over the pounding of my own heart. *This is fun.* I put my lips around him. He tasted good, salty and sweet. And my tongue loved the soft feel of his skin even more than my fingers. I slid my mouth down as far as I could go and wrapped my fingers and thumb around the rest of his shaft. I'd read about taking a guy all the way into your throat, but I thought I might gag and I didn't want to spoil the moment. I pulled my lips up and down while my fingers followed. I held his nuts in my other hand, fingering the sack, feeling the shape of his balls. Mr. Lawrence pressed against the back of his chair, his fingers gripping his thighs as if he feared touching me. I looked up in the shadows and saw his mouth hanging open and his eyes closed.

Suddenly his cock twitched in my mouth and I could feel his balls moving in my hand. I moved my lips and hand faster and soon he pumped my mouth full of jism. I swallowed, but he just kept spurting. I didn't want to let any get on our clothes and cause trouble, so I just kept my lips tight around his cock, swallowing when I could, until he finally stopped. His whole body sort of went limp in his chair. I licked him all over to make sure I hadn't missed any sticky stuff. Then, I stood up, straddled his legs again, and kissed him.

"Sabrina, why did you do that?" he asked when we finally released our lip lock.

"'Cause I wanted to."

"And, what do you want now?" His tone seemed rather mournful for a guy who'd just gotten a blow job from an eighteen-year-old virgin.

I nuzzled his neck with my nose and whispered. "I want you to fuck me."

"Sabrina, I could lose my job." His hands found their way under my blouse and he stroked my back with one and caressed my hoo hoos with the other.

I'm thinking, *Hey, you twit, I'm giving you my cherry and all you can think about is your stupid job?* I didn't say anything out loud, afraid I would scare him even more if he knew I was a virgin. Instead I licked my way up his neck and behind his ear. He pushed my blouse and sweater up to expose my boobs and took one of them in his mouth, wrapping his tongue around my nipple. I pulled my tops up over my head and tossed them on his desk. Mr. Lawrence sucked on my left ta-ta with his mouth while his hand squeezed my right knocker. His other hand moved under my skirt, and fondled my hiney. I liked all this attention and I was getting wetter by the minute. I could feel his dick, still hanging outside his pants, twitching against my cunt lips.

Mr. Lawrence put his hands around my waist, picked me up, and set me on the desk. He pushed back my skirt and pulled apart my beaver.

"God, you're beautiful," he whispered and then he dove right in. Now, I've read lots about muff eating and I can tell you right now none of what I read did it justice. I hooked the heels of my saddle shoes on the desk so I could keep my legs spread wide, leaned back on my hands, and just sat there with my tongue hanging out and my eyes rolled back in my head.

He licked the outside of my hole and then lapped at my clit. He pushed his tongue into my virgin puss and I wondered if he would go deep enough to feel my cherry. Fortunately, if he did, it didn't stop him from going back to wrap his lips around my clitty. I could feel the juices dripping from my box while his tongue and lips sent me to heaven. When I started coming, the intensity of the feeling overwhelmed me. Compared to what I could do by playing with myself this was like the difference between a little model train set and a big freakin' locomotive engine. Mr. Lawrence didn't stop and neither did I. I finally had to clamp my hand over my own mouth 'cause I could no longer keep myself from screaming out loud and getting us both in trouble.

My whole body shook violently. I must have come for five whole minutes before Mr. Lawrence took his face from between my legs and pulled me back into his lap. He wrapped his arms tightly around me, flattening my breasts against the solid muscles of his chest, and I could feel the buttons of his shirt pressing into my skin. I still trembled a little and the walls of my passion hole spasmed like some kind of after-shock.

"I think you should go back to your room, now, Sabrina." His voice was hoarse and I could feel that his dick had gotten all hard again.

"That was wonderful, Mr. Lawrence." My voice was a little shaky too, but I was more determined than ever to have this hunk of a man take my cherry. "But I still want you to fuck me."

"God, please don't call me Mr. Lawrence at a time like this. My name is Robert."

"I still want you to fuck me, Robert." I unbuttoned his shirt and pushed it away from his shoulders. He had bristly black hairs covering his chest and I ran my fingers through them. I nibbled on his nip and he tightened his grip around me. I sucked at it and his breathing got heavier. Then, he stood up with me still in his lap and lay me across his desk, my sweater and blouse under my head like a pillow. He dropped his trousers and climbed up on top of me, his pelvis settling between my thighs. *Finally.*

Mr. Lawrence, Robert, covered my mouth with his and his tongue danced with mine. I sucked my own juices off his lips -- I tasted pretty good. Robert leaned on one arm while his other hand guided his big fat dick toward my cock-pit. I laced my fingers behind his neck and opened my legs wide. He pushed slowly into me and stopped, gasping, when the head of his penis pressed against my hymen. He started to pull back, but I held on tight, sucking his tongue deeper into my mouth, wrapping my legs around his waist, and crossing my ankles behind his back. For a moment, those clear blue eyes stared through to my very soul. He must have seen what he wanted, because all at once he jammed himself deep inside me. If my mouth hadn't been full of his tongue, I would have screamed for sure. I couldn't believe how much it hurt. It felt like he'd split me in two.

For a while, Robert didn't move. We just lay there, tangled up together, until the pain started to ease up a bit. I realized I'd done it. I was no longer a virgin. More importantly, I liked the feeling of his cock filling me up. I started to push my hips up toward him. As if he'd waited for that cue, Robert moved also. He pulled back until just the head of his dong was inside me and then pushed it all the way in again. Once I got over the pain, I got lost in the exquisite sensation of him pumping in and out of me. I clung to him with all my strength, trying to move my hips to match his rhythm. I could feel his balls slapping against my ass every time he thrust into me and he ground his pelvis into my clit. This time, I think my orgasm lasted more than ten minutes. I have no idea, but it seemed to go on forever.

My pussy kept spasming long after Robert pumped me full of his sticky jism. I could feel his come running down the crack of my ass and getting all over his calendar. Good thing March was almost over. We lay there, basking in the warmth of each other's bodies, and I started to think that maybe the rest of the term wasn't going to be so bad after all.

Arresting Development

By I.G. Frederick

I knew I hadn't exceeded the speed limit by more than five miles an hour when I saw the flashing blue lights behind me. *Shit*, I thought. *If I get a speeding ticket, my insurance rates will go up and I can barely afford that and the car payments now.* I'd gotten tired of driving around in a rusty heap of metal with an engine and finally broken down and borrowed money from my dad for a replacement.

The cop who stepped out of the squad was older, probably late thirties, and tall, at least six feet. His steel-grey eyes so mesmerized me, I think he asked for my driver's license and registration twice. The reality of what a ticket would do to my finances, strangled by my barely-over-minimum wage salary and college tuition, started to sink in again while he wrote down all my info.

"Tell you what," the officer looked at what he had written, "Bethany. I'll just give you a warning if you'll go out with me." He had a deep voice that sent chills down my spine.

Although he had a nice build, the cop had to have twenty years on me. And except for those eyes, his craggy face didn't exactly ring my chimes. His thick black hair was cut way too short and his skin was kind of blotchy. Plus, my dad would probably freak if he got wind of me dating an older man. My mom had died when I was four, so Dad tended to be over-protective. He probably thought I was still a virgin and I tried not to disillusion him. I just couldn't afford rent for my own place. Apartments in town were scarce and expensive.

I weighed my options. *How will Dad react to a speeding tick-et?* I knew he'd probably try something juvenile like ground-ing me for a month, and maybe even call in his car loan. As long as I lived under his roof, Dad figured he could still con-trol my life, despite the fact that I was eighteen.

I sized up the cop. Craggy face aside, he looked mighty fine in his blue uniform. *And what Dad doesn't know can't get me in trouble.* I agreed to meet him -- he said his name was Rick -- after work for coffee at a diner on the outskirts of town. Hopefully, there I wouldn't run into anyone I knew.

When I walked into the diner and saw that I'd arrived first, I took a seat in a booth in the back, where I was less likely to get spotted. Rick showed up wearing plain old blue jeans and a bulky, green sweater. *I guess he can't wear his uni-form all the time.* But, I was still pretty disappointed. Even out of uniform, Rick walked through the place like he owned it. Instead of sitting across the table, he scooted in beside me, so I had to move over to make room for him. After he sat down, the waitress poured us cups of barely drinkable coffee.

"I have a confession to make." Rick took a sip and didn't seem to mind the bitter brew. I guess cops get used to drink-ing all kinds of dreck. "I want you to know that I never in-tended to give you a ticket."

I poured sugar in my coffee and stirred, wondering ex-actly what I had gotten myself into.

"In this town, we usually don't stop anyone unless they're going at least ten miles over the limit." He spun the cup around and around with one hand. "I've seen you driving around in that snazzy blue convertible, your hair flying out behind you."

Before I bought the car, I'd always kept my hair, which hung halfway down my back, in a braid. But I liked the feeling of the wind blowing through it when I drove with the top down and had started wearing it loose. If I'd known that would get me stopped by a cop, I would have kept it plaited.

Rick half-turned so he could look me in the eye. "I have a weakness for women with long hair, especially ones with green eyes, although I didn't discover those until the traffic stop." He smiled which erased some of the crags and made his face almost appealing. "I know it's lame, but, I really wanted to meet you and I couldn't think of another way. I didn't want to scare off any of the clients by showing up at the rehab center."

I stared at him, my eyes widening when I realized he knew where I worked.

"Don't worry. I didn't really write up a warning." He misinterpreted my reaction. "I just copied down your name and address so I could get in touch with you if you wouldn't agree to meet with me tonight." Rick grabbed his cup and took a gulp. "And, I wouldn't have written you a ticket, even if you had said no." He put his hand on my knee.

I felt the heat rise in my cheeks and I clenched my fist. I wanted to leave, but the only way I could have gotten out of the booth was to crawl under the table. Rick had his leg pressed against mine and his hand drifted up and down the inside of my thigh, sending shivers up my spine. I hadn't had sex since I broke up with my boyfriend, Jim, when he decided to join the Army six months ago.

Despite my anger at the ticket deception, my pussy responded to Rick's caresses. I kind of lost track of the conversation at that point. I know we talked about our respective career choices and the disadvantages of living in a small city. But Rick's hand on my leg prevented me from paying much attention.

I wore one of my shorter skirts that hiked halfway up my thigh when I sat down and a blouse with the top three buttons undone to reveal what I admit is an impressive cleavage. Apparently, Rick liked what he saw and felt because the bulge in his jeans got bigger. I had to wonder just what he had hidden in his pants.

Somewhere between the second and third cups of coffee, Rick's fingers found their way up to my satin panties. *Can he feel the dampness?*. When the waitress came back to our table, I thought about ordering something to eat. But Rick waved her away, threw some dollar bills on the table, took my hand, and led me out to the parking lot. He had parked his squad car next to my convertible.

"I'm afraid I'm going to have to take you in, little lady," he said. His deep voice was teasing, but it added to the heat between my legs.

"But you can't arrest me officer, you're not even in uniform," I protested.

"Who said anything about arresting you?" Rick's hand had taken firm possession of my ass and he guided me toward the squad car. "Besides, a policeman is always an officer of the law even when he's not on duty."

Rick opened the back door of the squad car and waited until I got in before closing it. The back seat had no handles inside; I couldn't get out of the car until he let me. Rick drove out to a spot near the lake. When he turned off the engine the only things I could hear were crickets and frogs. Rick lowered all four windows about half way and then joined me in the back seat. He pulled me into his arms and kissed me. I could taste coffee on his tongue as it filled my mouth. Unable to resist, I reached up and ran my fingers through his thick black hair. I felt my pussy getting wetter by the second.

Rick undid more of my blouse buttons and his lips traced

a searing hot path from my mouth down the mound of my breasts. He unhooked my bra and I moaned when his tongue found my hardened nipple. His hand moved up under my skirt, his fingers pulled my panties aside, and he played with my button. My head swam. *Was this what he meant by "going out"? Am I doing this just to get out of a speeding ticket -- one that he never intended to write? Do I care?*

The man sent incredible sensations through my entire body. My ex-boyfriend had never made me feel like this. I let my hand slide slowly down Rick's chest until I reached the bulge in his pants. It had definitely gotten bigger. I tugged at the zipper, determined to see what he had to offer, but couldn't get it to budge. Rick laughed, unfastened his pants, and released himself from his shorts. I couldn't resist and slid off the seat onto my knees.

First I kissed it, covering the head and the shaft with moist little smacks. Rick sighed and ran his fingers through my hair. Then I licked it. I dragged my tongue up and down the shaft, around the head, and across his balls. He tasted so good, I just couldn't get enough. Finally, I took as much of him as I could in my mouth, sliding him in and out of my lips. Rick moaned. His fingers tangled in my hair and his hips bucked up toward my face. I thought he would come in my mouth, but he tugged on my hair and pulled my face back up to his.

With his mouth firmly clamped onto mine, Rick managed to roll on a condom he'd produced from his pocket. Then he lifted me up, positioned my hips, and oh so slowly, impaled me. I planted my knees up on the seat and Rick cupped his hands around my ass, guiding me up and down. His mouth moved down my neck and fastened itself onto one tit. That sent me. I shook and cried out as my pussy pulsated in one humongous orgasm. I had never come that hard or that long before. I was still throbbing when Rick pulled me tight against him and cried out.

We just sat there for a while, wrapped in each other's arms, until Rick went soft and slipped out. Then he kissed me and said: "I was right -- long hair, cool car, you are one red-hot babe."

I felt way too good to even think about being angry any-more.

"I want to see you again, Bethany." Rick let his fingers drift through my hair all the way to the ends.

I pouted. "Only if you wear your uniform next time." The thought of having sex with a cop in uniform made me hot all over again.

Rick just grinned. "Tell you what. Tomorrow, you head south of town at eight-thirty. Make sure you put your car's top down. Take Route 53."

"And then what?"

"That's all you need to know, babe." He kissed the side of my neck.

"But where will we meet?"

"You leave the details to me," he muttered, his breath hot on my skin.

When I got home, I avoided my dad's questions by mak-ing noises about hanging with the other girls from work and went straight to my room claiming exhaustion. I was so ex-cited, though, I had trouble sleeping. I had to finger my clit, while remembering the taste of Rick in my mouth, until I came again.

$\mathcal{A}$

The next day, I found it hard to concentrate on my work. I alternated between berating myself for having sex with someone I'd just met, complaining about still living with my dad, and getting wet wondering what Rick had in store for the evening. Finally, I took myself into the rest room and had a long conversation with the mirror. "You agreed you would stay at home until you finished college so you didn't have to borrow a fortune for school. You decided to make a career out of helping people even though you knew the pay was shit. You're not ready for another serious relationship right now, you're still hurting over Jim. The sex rocks and there's nothing wrong with an unattached, eighteen-year-old college student indulging in some NSA entertainment."

I didn't look convinced, but I still made an excuse to leave the house after supper and head toward Route 53. When I saw blue lights flashing behind me, I pulled over to the side of the deserted road. I'd driven at least ten miles south of town and probably several from the nearest house. I waited for a cop to ask for my driver's license.

Instead, a bright flashlight blinded me and Rick's deep, stern voice told me: "Get out of the car and keep your hands where I can see them." He opened the door and I did as I was told, my pussy so wet my panties were soaked by the time I swung my legs out and rose to my feet.

"Put your hands on the hood of the car, your feet back and spread them as wide as you can." I couldn't move until I reminded myself that the voice, and everything else in the uniform, belonged to the same man who had given me the ride of my life the night before.

I closed the car door, placed my hands on the warm hood, and inched my feet back and apart. In this position I couldn't move without losing my balance. He turned off the beam and I heard the big metal flashlight sliding back into its belt loop. I felt two hands on either side of my bare ankle working their way up to my thigh. Then the side of his hand jabbed between my legs and I shuddered. Rick couldn't help feel how wet my panties were, but he took his hand away and repeated his pat down on the other leg. This time, though, his hand stayed between my legs for a minute, his fingers wiggling until I almost couldn't stand it. I tried to ride his hand, but he pulled away and patted my butt and up my waist.

He thoroughly examined my breasts, pinching my nipples, hard. When he released them, he grabbed my right wrist, tugged that hand behind my back, and snapped on a cuff, the metal cold against my skin. He pulled my other hand behind my back, forcing me to lean against the car hood, and secured my wrist with an ominous clicking of the cuff locking into position.

"Hmmmm, nothing. I'm afraid I'm going to have to do a strip search and a complete body cavity examination." Rick managed to make his voice sound menacing, but I could hear his ragged breathing. He pulled me to an upright position, unbuttoned my shirt, and unfastened the front clasp of my bra, pushing both back over my arms.

I had debated about changing into something sexy after work, but had decided to avoid a wardrobe confrontation with my dad. I still wore a hippie-style peasant blouse and denim skirt.

In the flashing light from his squad, Rick made a show of searching my clothing for contraband and then he grabbed my tits, his fingers probing. Every inch of my upper torso succumbed to his rough scrutiny, so delicious I trembled with excitement. I wanted him so badly, but I enjoyed the anticipation too much to rush him. He undid my skirt and pushed it and my panties down to the ground. I stood naked in the blue light wearing only my Teva sandals, my arms pinned behind my back by the cuffs and my own clothing. As he rose, Rick's fingers explored the skin of my legs, my ass and my belly. Everywhere but where I wanted to feel them the most -- inside my pussy lips. When he finally stood, Rick pulled me roughly against him, his lips covering mine, his tongue exploring my mouth. I could feel his belt with all the leather pouches for equipment, pressing against my skin. His badge left an imprint in my shoulder. I was panting.

After his unsuccessful "search" of my mouth, Rick turned me around, pushing my bare breasts against the still-warm hood of my car. He worked two fingers into my wet pussy and wiggled them around while I pushed my hips back toward him.

He leaned over and whispered in my ear. "Guess my fingers just aren't long enough to do a proper search. Fortunately, I have another tool at my disposal."

He pulled his hand free and I heard a zipper pull down and a condom package rip open. I shivered, thinking about his cock probing my wet pussy. If I wasn't leaning on the car, my legs wouldn't have supported my weight -- my knees felt so weak. Rick pushed into me, exploring every inch of me. He leaned forward and grabbed my breasts in his hands, pinching my nipples as he pulled back and then slammed into me again. I couldn't believe how much getting taken by a cop in uniform -- who still wore his gun, ammunition belt, and night stick -- turned me on.

"Nothing here either," Rick whispered in my ear. "One more cavity to search."

I hesitated. I had never taken it up the ass. But I desperately needed to come and Rick had already pulled out of my pussy. I heard the snap of a rubber glove and felt cold lube as he eased his fingers inside my ass. Just what else did he have stashed in all those little leather pockets?

"Guess my fingers aren't long enough, again." He leaned against my back, his breath hot on my neck. The glove hit the asphalt with a plop.

He rubbed the head of his rubber-encased cock, against my virgin ass. Inch by inch he slowly eased it in, stopping to let me get used to the feeling, until he was balls deep. Rick pulled almost all the way out, reached around and kneaded my clit between his thumb and finger. I pushed my hips back into his pelvis and Rick shoved all the way into me again. I screamed as the orgasm convulsed my entire body. Rick kept sliding in and out of me -- one hand fingering my clit, the other massaging one tit -- until he came big time. We both splayed across the hood of my car, quivering and panting, unable to move. Finally Rick eased himself out of me, and pulled me gently into his arms. He held me, the lights from his squad still flashing around us, until I stopped trembling and we both were breathing normally.

"Babe, you just made one of my favorite fantasies a reality." He kissed me. "I want to pull you over every night."

I just looked up into his craggy face and grinned. Nothing could make me happier.

"You wanna go get something to eat?" he asked.

I nodded. Rick removed the handcuffs and helped me pull my clothes back on. He walked me to the door of my car and stood there until I fastened my seat belt and started the engine. Then I followed him into town to the diner, wondering what tomorrow night would bring.

Jail Bait

By I. G Frederick

After seeing him almost for six months, Serena decided Joshua was the man she wanted to take her cherry. But unlike every high school boy she'd ever dated, he didn't feel her up every chance he got, or insinuate that her lack of interest in having sex the third time they went out meant she was frigid. Even when she confided her most perverted fantasies, even after she told him she'd started taking birth control pills, he only kissed her on the cheek and said, "You're still jail bait, Babe."

Tomorrow her parents planned a huge family gathering at Devil's Lake in honor of her eighteenth birthday. But Joshua promised her that tonight would be even more special. She smoothed down the elegant little black dress that Joshua had bought her as an early birthday present. It fit like a glove, showing off her slender figure and revealing lots of cleavage and leg. Leaving the ladies room, she found him waiting in a corner booth overlooking the bay.

He stood up when she approached, ruggedly handsome

with straight chestnut hair and a muscular chest visible under his black polo shirt. She slid in so she sat between him and the wall.

"I've ordered you a virgin Piña Colada." He picked up the menu, but was interrupted almost immediately by the waiter setting drinks in front of them.

Serena sipped at the delightful combination of pineapple and coconut. She would never have known to ask for such a concoction. Dating an older man had so very many side benefits.

The waiter had returned without his tray and stood in front of their table, his hands behind his back. Joshua ordered the duck in lemon sauce. They both turned to her and the waiter said, "And for your daughter, sir?"

Joshua raised one eyebrow above the other. "She's not my daughter."

"Beg pardon, Sir." The waiter's facial expression didn't change. "What would you like for dinner, Miss?"

Serena was a bit taken aback by the prices, but since Joshua didn't seem to mind, she ordered the scallops in beurre blanc sauce. When the waiter left, Joshua lifted his martini glass and she clinked it with hers. He scooted closer and kissed the back of her neck. She melted against his shoulder. "You look beautiful in that dress. Thanks for forgoing undies," he whispered in her ear.

She blushed and buried her face against his neck.

"Our little secret." He took a sip of his drink from his right hand while his left drifted across her bare shoulders and pulled her closer. He toyed with her long, reddish brown hair, wrapping strands around his fingers then letting them pull free..

The heat between Serena's legs spread up to her chest, meeting the blush that had crept from her face to her neck. By the time the waiter set plates in front of them, the only thing she wanted to put in her mouth was Joshua's cock. She knew better than to suggest it, though. Dating horny high school boys who rarely took no for an answer, she'd gotten rather good at blow jobs. But Joshua always turned down her offers to demonstrate her skills on him. Since she couldn't have the meat she wanted, she settled for the delectable scallops with couscous. Joshua stole one of her scallops and shared tastes of his lemony duck with her.

Despite her protests that she was stuffed, Joshua insisted they share a berry cobbler with ice cream for dessert. By the time it arrived, they were the only patrons still in the restaurant. Staff had cleared and reset all the tables and she could hear a vacuum cleaner operating on the other side of the wall. She enjoyed the smooth creamy vanilla combined with tart berries and flaky crust. But she left most of the treat for Joshua.

When they emerged from the restaurant, the full moon had risen high in the sky and summer's heat had disappeared with the sun. Serena shivered and Joshua removed his blazer, wrapping it around her. With one arm across her shoulders, he led her away from the almost-empty parking lot and toward the bay.

They wandered along the spit and Serena could see the light of a bonfire burning near the cliff below the highway. When they reached it, she saw that two large driftwood logs had been pulled up to the cliff to provide a triangular shelter from the ocean breeze. A large blanket covered the sand between the fire and one log and a cooler sat between two camp chairs on the opposite side. Joshua glanced at his watch and guided Serena over to the chairs. "Thirsty?" He pointed at the cooler and sat down.

She shook her head.

"Cold?"

"Not now." She smiled and held her hands out toward the fire.

Joshua picked up a large gray Thermos® bottle from the sand next to the cooler. "Hot chocolate?"

She shrugged. "Sure, why not." Although the fire and his

jacket kept the chill away, Serena admitted to herself that she still wasn't exactly warm.

Steam drifted up from the plastic cups as Joshua filled them, handing one to her and putting the stopper back on the bottle before taking a sip from his. Serena held her cup with both hands, soaking in the warmth, and blew across the top, inhaling the rich aroma. The blanket indicated Joshua had more in mind than sharing cocoa, but he certainly didn't act like it.

The crackle of the fire and the lapping of waves on the sand punctuated the silence which neither seemed interested in breaking. Joshua kept looking at his watch while they sipped their drinks. Finally he grinned, his white teeth glistening in the firelight. He set his cup on the cooler, knelt in front of her, and ran his hands up her calves, until they reached her skirt which he edged above her knees. "It's midnight. Happy birthday, Babe." He kissed the insides of first one thigh and then the other just below her skirt. Serena gasped.

"Are you ready to become a woman tonight?"

She nodded enthusiastically. *Finally*.

Joshua rose up and kissed her, one hand behind her neck, the other sliding under her skirt. Their tongues twisted together in a cocoa-laced dance. His lips left hers and crept along her jaw to her throat, down her neck, until he buried his face in the cleavage exposed by the low-cut dress. Serena was panting and pushed off the jacket that had suddenly become too warm. He eased the straps of her dress down her shoulders, exposing her bare breasts to the chill air. With his tongue, he caressed her nipples until her hips involuntarily lifted off the chair. The heat between her legs had rushed above the temperature of the bonfire and she felt as if she was melting down there.

Leaving her nipples moist and erect, Joshua moved his mouth down to her legs again. He pulled gently, until her hips balanced on the edge of the chair. Pushing her skirt up as far as it would go, he kissed his way toward her hot, moist pussy. Holding her lips open with his fingers, he stuck out his tongue and slowly ran it from the bottom of her slit to her clit. A squeak escaped Serena's mouth and she heard it as if it had come from someone else. Joshua licked again and Serena slid further down in the chair, her knees finding their way up his arms to rest on his shoulders.

Each time his tongue caressed her virgin puss, the sensation became more intense. Her breathing became labored and she gripped the chair arms. Then he captured her clit with his lips and Serena exploded, her whole body shaking. She could feel herself gushing all over his face and worried that he would get upset with her.

"Such sweet honey," he muttered without emerging from between her legs. He licked and sucked until she shook again, crying out his name.

Joshua rose up, pulling her face toward his with one hand behind her neck. Serena hesitated, but let him press his lips to hers. *Not a bad taste, actually*, she thought with relief. No wonder he'd called it honey.

He stood up, pulled her to her feet, then lifted her in his arms. "Kick off your sandals." When she did, he wiped the sand off her feet with his handkerchief before setting her on the blanket. Then he removed his shoes, one at a time, stripping off his socks and placing his bare feet carefully on the blanket. "Don't want to roll around in sand." He looked at her from her naked breasts to her exposed bush with the dress still around her waist. "My God, you're beautiful." He held out his hands. "I've waited so long for this."

Stepping close to her, he pulled the dress over her head and dropped it on the blanket. Serena fell to her knees and fumbled with his belt, her hands shaking with anticipation, until she unbuckled it. While she got his dockers unzipped, he stripped off his shirt. She pulled down his slacks and he stood naked before her, the biggest cock she had ever seen pointing straight at her face. Serena stared at it, her eyes wide. The boys she'd sucked had miniature peckers compared to his and she panicked at the thought of taking him inside her virgin twat.

"Don't worry, Babe. I'll be gentle," he said, as if he could read her mind.

Serena took a deep breath and wrapped her lips around the head. He tasted so good and he wasn't the only one who had waited eagerly for tonight. She slid her lips as far as they would go which was only about half way down his cock. Wrapping her hand around the rest of his shaft, Serena slid her mouth back and forth. She discovered if she relaxed her throat to let him all the way in, she could get far enough for his pubic hair to tickle her nose. She breathed through her nose to avoid gagging. Joshua ran his fingers through her hair, but didn't push her head into his crotch or try to face fuck her.

Her jaw cramped up, so Serena rubbed his cock against her cheeks and pushed her tits up against either side of it. When she took him back in her mouth, she could tell he was close. She fisted the base of his cock with one hand, fondled his balls with the other, and sucked on his glans for all she was worth until he shot loads of hot, sweet cum into her mouth. She gulped it all down and then licked him from pubes to tip to make sure she hadn't missed any.

He dropped onto his knees besides her. "You weren't bragging, you really are good." He kissed her, wrapping his arms around her, pressing her breasts against his heated skin. Joshua pulled her down onto the blanket, laying next to her, his arms and legs wrapped around her, kissing her lips, her neck, her earlobes, stroking her hips, her ass, her breasts with his fingers. The distant roar of the ocean joined the sound of her heart and Jack's pounding in her ears.

Easing her onto her back, he gently pushed her legs apart and lay between them. He held his cock, hard again, in one hand and opened her lips with the other. Serena gasped as the tip entered her, pressing against her hymen. Joshua put one hand on either side of her face and looked into her eyes, the flicker of the firelight reflected in his irises. "Ready?"

She nodded and he pressed his lips hard against her, thrust his tongue deep into her mouth, and pushed himself into her. The sharp pain lasted only for a moment and she pushed her hips up into him. He pulled back and thrust again. With her mouth and cunt full of him, the tension started building in her clit again. She wiggled in delight and Joshua chuckled, pressing himself closer to her, gripping her ass cheeks. Serena tightened her arms around his back, holding on as she exploded yet again.

When she finally stopped trembling, Joshua rolled off of her. To her chagrin, she noted that the camp chairs had moved to the blanket side of the fire and that they were now both occupied with naked men. Serena blushed.

Joshua rose up onto his knees. "Babe, I want you to meet a couple of my frat brothers."

She pushed herself into a sitting position, cross-legged on the blanket with one hand holding each breast.

"This is Robert, we only call him Bob if we want to piss him off."

The man on her right stood, put one hand in front and one hand behind his waist and bowed. "Very pleased to make your acquaintance, Miss." He dropped to his knees and held one hand out to her. He had silky blond hair that brushed his shoulders and a pencil thin mustache. In the firelight, she could see a few strands of blond hair scattered across his chest and a v-shaped forest of them surrounding his very erect penis. Keeping one arm across her nipples, Serena lifted her right hand in his direction. He raised it to his lips and kissed each of her fingers in turn.

"And, this is Sid." Serena tore her eyes away from Robert to look at the naked man with curly read hair both on his head and at the cleft of his legs.

Although neither man was as big as Joshua, they both made her former boyfriends look inadequate. *I'll never date a high school boy again*, Serena promised herself.

Sid held out his hand until Serena reluctantly let go of her breasts and allowed him to kiss her fingers as well.

Joshua had maneuvered behind her. He cupped her perky tits in his large hands and kissed the back of her neck. "Robert and Sid are here to help me make your, as you call it, most perverted fantasy come true."

Serena's eyes opened wider and her gaze drifted from one to the other. Both grinned at her.

"Would you like that?" Jack's hot breath tickled her skin. She nodded. "Oh, yes, please."

Joshua chuckled again and nodded to Sid. He stretched out on his back near them and Joshua guided Serena into place, straddling his hips. Sid held his cock for her so she could sit on it.. When it slid inside her, he gasped and smiled at her.

Joshua had her lean forward on her hands. Sid caressed her tits and she felt a cold finger pressed against her butt hole. "Relax, Babe."

Serena took a deep breath as Joshua eased first one then two lube-slicked fingers up inside her. He withdrew and she felt him push his cock against her virgin ass. Sid waited until Joshua had eased himself inside her then with one hand on each of her hips, moved his own cock in and out of her puss. Serena moaned, balancing on her hands and knees, delighting in the sensation of having both her holes completely and utterly filled.

A hand stroked her hair and Serena looked up to see Robert's cock pointing at her mouth. She smiled, Joshua had gotten every detail of her fantasy exactly right. She opened her mouth just wide enough for Robert to slide it in. She was able to relax enough to get most of him down her throat without the aid of her hands.

The three men moved in unison, pounding into her with the rhythm of the waves hitting the sand. Joshua cupped her breasts in his hands, Robert played with her hair while he fucked her mouth, and Sid rubbed her clit with his thumb as he pushed up into her. Their breath came in short, quick gasps. Serena lost track of time and only the constant hammering of the surf kept her aware of where she was. Every inch of her body throbbed with pleasure even as she ached from over stimulation.

Every man's touch radiated through her body, settling in her clit. Sid's thumb pushed the intensity of the sensations to their peak. The shaking started in her toes and weakened her knees and elbows until she collapsed on top of Sid. The men kept moving in and out of her while she screamed, the sound muffled by Robert's cock filling her mouth and lost in the ocean's roar.

Robert came first, pulling out and spraying sticky cum all over her face. She licked her lips. He wasn't as sweet as Joshua, but she still enjoyed the taste. After a few more strokes, Sid and Joshua grunted and shot their load at the same time, sandwiching her between them while she trembled and twitched.

They held her until she could blink again. Sid had shrunk out of her by then. Joshua, eased himself out of her ass and stretched out next to her. She rolled off of Sid to lie between them and the two pressed up against her. Robert, sitting perpendicular to them all, pillowed her head on his thigh. Serena's cunt still throbbed, but the rest of her had stopped spasming.

Joshua started and the other two joined in singing, ever so softly: "Happy birthday to you, happy birthday to you, happy birthday beautiful Serena, happy birthday to you."

Acknowledgements

This book would not have reached your hands without the help of many dear friends and colleagues. I thank my readers and supporters, especially Cindy, my proofreader, editor and best friend, and Anne Denbok who bought the first short story I sold, as well as "Teacher's Pet Pussy." Thanks also to all those who have served me, well and ill, over the years. I have learned something from each one of you and I hope that you find what you seek.

Other fiction

by I.G. Frederick includes:

Complicated Couplings

Four sexy stories about tangled twosomes

"If You Love Someone" — Tara leaves her husband to move in with Nathan, but he abandons her after a few months. When he returns, begging her to take him back, life and love look very different.

"Commiserate" — The same man dumped them both. When they commiserate, they discover more in common than an ex-boyfriend.

"Passion's Price" — Richard steals Gina's heart from three thousand miles away. But, when he moves across the country, her intensity and passion for life drive him away.

"Lunchtime Lover" — Both married, they started their affair with the promise never to fall in love. Then Lisa's divorce becomes final.

www.eroticawriter.net/ComplicatedCouplings.html

Cougar Conquests

Beautiful older women on the prowl and the sweet young cubs captured by their allure

"Benjamin" — *A chance meeting at a munch in a tiny town leads Benjamin to an opportunity for training. But, Lady Gina tries to end the relationship rather than emotionally torture herself.*

"Festival of Eros" — *The handsome young man followed her around all evening, behaving like the perfect submissive ... until she learned his identity.*

"Paddles" — *A biker bar with no bikers? The decor, name, and patrons of a bar in a small Eastern Oregon town puzzle William who just stopped in for a beer. Then the owner introduces him to the secrets of this very special tavern.*

"Starting Over" - *When her pet walked out on her, she stayed away from parties because it hurt to watch other women playing with their toys. But, a friend coerces her into attending a unique event.*

"The Cougar and the College Boys" — *Alone in the woods, hours from Portland, Tess discovers four college friends staying in a nearby cabin. The boys invite her to share their campfire, their dinner, and ...*

www.eroticawriter.net/CougarConquests.html

Dommemoir

WARNING:

This book changes women's attitudes about relationship dynamics, forever.

In Geneviéve's journey of discovery she dabbles in the BDSM lifestyle which forces her to recognize and acknowledge her true nature. Her memoir, woven together with that of a male slave, draws the reader into an intense odyssey of sexual expression triumphing over sexual repression while delivering fascinating insight about a different kind of love.

"The aptly titled Dommemoir *delivers on so many levels... It quickly sucks you in and envelopes you in the bondage of its spell...* Dommemoir *is a character study that breathes complex and compelling life into its hero, the devastating Lady Geneviéve and the fortunate submissives who worship at her feet... placing you in the delicious bondage of its dark and compelling landscape..."*

Larry Brooks, USA Today *bestselling author of* Darkness Bound **and** Bait and Switch

www.eroticawriter.net/Dommemoir.html

Eleanor & Mick

A journey of seoxual exploration and insight

In five sizzling hot stories, Eleanor seeks refuge in a small town on the Oregon Coast and befriends her younger neighbor. He captures first her heart and then her submission, taking her on a journey of sexual exploration and insight.

"Salt for His Wounds" — When Eleanor's ex-husband shows up begging for a second chance, she asks her young, gorgeous next door neighbor for a favor and Mick takes advantage of the opportunity.

"The Mercantile" — Eleanor attributes Mick's detachment to the difference in their ages, but Mick confesses a need for kink. Afraid of losing him, Eleanor reluctantly consents to bondage and pain.

"The Things We Do for Love" — When her gorgeous girlfriend visits Eleanor on the coast, Mick's obvious attraction troubles her. But, Liz only has eyes for Eleanor.

"Paid in Full" — Mick's army buddy finds Eleanor hot and makes a deal with Mick. But, if Mick really loved Eleanor would he let another man have sex with her?

"Renovations" — After Mick spends a month renovating their garage, Eleanor discovers he built in a few surprises.

www.eroticawriter.net/EleanorMick.html

Family Dynamics

Six sultry stories exploring sexuality in Dominant/submissive liaisons

"'Aunt' Grace" — Jen needed a place to stay in Portland and turned to her father's stepsister. But, she found so much more than she ever dreamed possible with her "Aunt" Grace. Second Place, NLA:I John Preston Short Story Award.

"Leather Family" — Kyle needs his own boy. Jacques would do almost anything to find a place in a Leather Family. But, Kyle serves a female Master.

"Searching" — Two dominants love each other, but need someone who submits to them both. Just how far will young Jeremy go to serve the lovely Lady Theresa?

"Taking Control" — To free the woman she loves from a horrid sadist's perverted games, Melanie must set aside her own aversion to men.

"Family Ties" — When her slave's ex faces eviction, Katherine offers refuge. But can Naomi pay the price?

"Said the Unicorn" — Tessa dedicates herself to her Master's service, so his determination to add another woman to their family devastates her.

www.eroticawriter.net/FamilyDynamics.html

Fork In The Road:

Changing people's lives, and relationships in three pairs of sexy stories

"Said the Unicorn" — Tessa dedicates herself to her Master's service, so his determination to add another woman to their family devastates her.

"Proposals" — The evening appears perfectly arranged for him to pop the question. But, Christopher's proposition takes Geraldine on an unanticipated sexual adventure.

"Winners & Losers" — When he finally walks away from the blackjack table, Jeffrey finds someone worth gambling on.

www.eroticawriter.net/ForkinRoad.html

Ladies in Love
Six sizzling stories of Lesbian Lust

"Empty Seat" — Laura offers Alex a nightcap as thanks for help with a presentation to a prospective client. But they never order drinks.

"'Aunt' Grace" — Jen needed a place to stay in Portland and turned to her father's stepsister. But, she found so much more than she ever dreamed possible

with her "Aunt" Grace. Second Place, NLA:I John Preston Short Story Award.

"Spa Date" — Dismayed that she introduced Sam to the woman who betrayed her, Julie tries to fix her up again.

"Taking Control" — To free the woman she loves from a horrid sadist's perverted games, Melanie must set aside her own aversion to men.

"Dental School" — How can Cindy flirt with the beautiful blonde dental instructor while her mother propositions the student examining her teeth on Cindy's behalf?

"Commiserate" — The same man dumped them both. When they commiserate, they discover more in common than an ex-boyfriend.

www.eroticawriter.net/LadiesinLove.html

Lessons Learned
Sometimes you need more than love

Four sizzling hot FemDom love stories about women who come to terms with their dominant sides and discover that makes them more attractive to the men they love.

"Tea Party" — What if the first time your best friend drags you to a FemDom "Tea Party" you see your former boyfriend serving canapes naked?

"Blind Date" — How do you respond when you find

your ex-husband hanging out at the restaurant where you planned to meet your "Blind Date"?

"To Serve" — *If you love a vanilla woman and you only want "To Serve," how do you introduce her to the lifestyle without scaring her away?*

"Change in View" — *What if a "Change in View" alters the attitude of the man you mentored so he could find his perfect Mistress?*

www.eroticawriter.net/LessonsLearned.html

ℒove ℋurts

but in a good way
five steamy stories about the dark side of love

"B&D Trainee" —*Online, Xavier promised to make his B&D fantasies come true. But, had he jumped in over his head?*

"Knife Play" — *Seeking a knife he saw online, Jack inadvertently found himself in a room full of pain and bondage contraptions. He almost turned around and left, but a beautiful woman taught him a different way to appreciate blades.*

"Pussy Whipped" — *Eric knew nothing about BDSM, but purchased a ticket to a fundraiser to help out his friends. When Miranda asks him to "play," he discovers exactly what those four letters mean.*

"The Auction" — He attended the auction with only one goal — to acquire a very special whip. But an offer to try it out proved irresistible and he discovered sometimes events, and women, can exceed one's expectations.

"FemDom Fairy Tale" — A FemDom's offhand remark about a photograph at an erotic art show draws a handsome man's attention. But, when two dominants find each other attractive, which one chooses to kneel?

www.eroticawriter.net/LoveHurts.html

Second Chances

Six sexy stories about getting a second shot at the gold ring

"Back to School" — An admin error forces Jordan and Dennis to share a dorm room. Older than their classmates, they decide to stick together. But Jordan's past threatens to keep them apart.

"Gordon" — When the cover model of her latest book walks into the coffee shop where she writes, Lenore embarrassingly calls him by her character's name. His reaction confounds her.

"Spa Date" — Dismayed that she introduced Sam to the woman who betrayed her, Julie tries to fix her up again.

"Salt for His Wounds" — When Eleanor's ex-husband shows up begging for a second chance, she asks her young, gorgeous next door neighbor for a favor. Mick takes advantage of the opportunity.

"Proposal — Tangled Webs" — The evening appears perfectly arranged for him to pop the question. But, Christopher's proposition takes Geraldine on an unanticipated sexual adventure.

"Starting Over" — When her pet walked out on her, she stayed away from parties because it hurt to watch other women playing with their toys. But, a friend coerces her into attending a unique event.

www.eroticawriter.net/SecondChances.html

When Two's Not Enough

Seven sexy ménage stories

"Tribal Fusion" — Whenever and wherever he dances, Dominic collects propositions, but the Lady Lenore's proposal takes him by surprise.

"Two Brothers" — A divorcée in a flashy sports car attracts the attention of two young virgin brothers visiting the "big" city of Boise.

"Honeymoon" — Although she expected to honeymoon aboard a cruise ship, Allison finds herself sailing on a private yacht staffed by an incredibly beautiful couple. Believing her new husband wants to hide his older, less attractive wife, makes it difficult to enjoy the hedonistic delights offered in paradise.

"Jail Bait" — Serena wants Joshua to pop her cherry,

but he won't touch her because of her age. When her birthday finally makes it legal, he arranges for a very special celebration.

"Nikki's Birthday" — Even someone happy in a monogamous relationship might find the gift of a hot, new toy for an evening of decadence incredibly exciting. (Inspired by a real birthday present given to a lovely little bi-sexual, genderqueer slave.)

"Market Boy" — When a beautiful Domme offers Jack the opportunity to serve at a party for her friends, he responds too quickly and too eagerly, getting more than he bargained for.

"The Cougar and the College Boys" — Alone in the woods, hours from Portland, Tess discovers four college friends staying in a nearby cabin. The boys invite her to share their campfire, their dinner, and ...

www.eroticawriter.net/TwoNotEnough.html

Or visit
http://eroticawriter.net/
to find links to individual stories
and additional collections
and